Olwen
finds her
Wings

The illustrations in this book were created using plant-based watercolours.

First published by Fukuinkan Shoten Publishers, Inc., Tokyo, Japan
in 2009 under the title *The Little Owl*
First published in English by Floris Books, Edinburgh in 2021
Story © 2009 Nora Surojegin. Illustrations © 2009 Pirkko-Liisa Surojegin
English version © 2021 Floris Books. All rights reserved. No part of this
publication may be reproduced without the prior permission of
Floris Books, Edinburgh www.florisbooks.co.uk

British Library CIP data available
ISBN 978-178250-712-3
Printed in Poland through Hussar

 Floris Books supports sustainable forest management by
printing this book on materials made from wood that
comes from responsible sources and reclaimed material

MIX
Paper from
responsible sources
FSC® C015559
FSC
www.fsc.org

Olwen
finds her
Wings

Nora Surojegin and Pirkko-Liisa Surojegin

Floris Books

Deep in a frosty forest, a family of owls lived happily in their treetop home.

All except Olwen, the youngest owl. Olwen was not happy.

"I'm bored with sitting on this branch all day long," Olwen grumbled to her brothers and sister. "What else can I do?"

"Soon you'll find out what you can do," said Mama owl.

But Olwen wasn't listening. She had spotted a creature leaping along the ground far below. Hopping around in the snow looked like lots of fun!

"Mama, can I leap in the snow too?" she cried.

Mama was a wise old owl. "Go, little one, and try something new."

When Olwen reached the ground, the creature stopped hopping and stared at her.

"Hello!" Olwen cheeped. "Can I be a Hopfoot just like you?"

"I'm not a Hopfoot, I'm a hare," the animal snuffled. "I can leap a long way with my strong legs. You can't do what I can do."

"Yes I can!" chirped Olwen.

She lifted her feet and tried to leap...

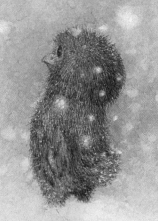

But her legs were much too short.

"No, I can't do what you can do," said Olwen sadly.

"You'll soon find out what you can do," said the
hare before he sprang away into the forest.

Just then, Olwen heard a growl.

Sharp claws crunched the snow in front of her.
Olwen looked up… and up… and up.

"Hello!" Olwen hooted. "Can I be a Growlmouth just like you?"

"I'm not a Growlmouth, I'm a bear," the animal grunted. "I can roar with my loud voice. You can't do what I can do."

"Yes I can!" chirped Olwen.

She took a deep breath and tried to roar…

But all that came out was a tiny tweet.
"No, I can't do what you can do," said Olwen sadly.

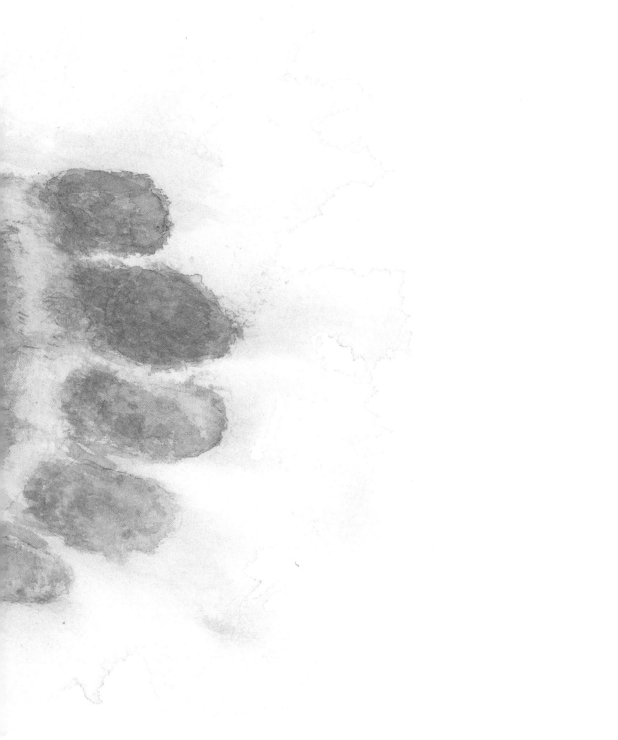

"You'll soon find out what you can do," said the bear.
"Let me give you a helping hand…"
And with a friendly chuckle and one swipe of her
paw, the bear launched Olwen into the air.
WHEE!

PLOP!

"Well, that didn't help!" Olwen squawked when she was the right way up again. "I still don't know what I can do."

She fluffed her feathers and shuffled through the snow.
Just then she heard a pattering sound high up above and
suddenly…

PLONK!

A pinecone fell down and hit her on the head.
Olwen looked up.

A furry face peered down.
Olwen slowly climbed the tree to find out
more about this curious creature.

"Hello!" Olwen tweeted. "Can I be a Patterpaw just like you?"

"I'm not a Patterpaw, I'm a squirrel," the animal chattered. "I can scamper along branches with my quick feet. You can't do what I can do."

"Yes I can!" chirped Olwen.

She dug in her talons and tried to scamper…

But she was much too slow.

"No, I can't do what you can do," said
Olwen sadly.

"You'll soon find out what you can do,"
called the squirrel as he jumped away.

"The only thing I've found out," Olwen hooted gloomily, "is that I can't do anything."

"That's not true!" hooted Mama as she landed next to Olwen. "You can do lots of wonderful things."

"But I can't leap like a hare, roar like a bear or scamper like a squirrel, Mama," squawked Olwen.

"That's true. But you, little Olwen, can do something none of those creatures can," replied Mama. "All you need to do is spread your wings and jump…"

"I can fly!" Olwen hooted happily.

"Wonderful, Olwen, you found
your wings!" called Mama as they
soared through the frosty forest.

When they arrived home, Olwen's brothers and
sister were wide-eyed with wonder.

"I can fly!" Olwen said proudly. "I can show you
how to find your wings too!"

"Tomorrow, little ones," murmured Mama.
"Now it is time to rest."

But Olwen was already fast asleep, dreaming of
all the places her wonderful wings would take her.

About the Author and Illustrator

Pirkko-Liisa Surojegin is a well-known Finnish children's book artist, renowned for her delicate and beautiful style. Among many other books, Pirkko-Liisa illustrated *An Illustrated Kalevala*, an award-winning adaptation of the Finnish epic.

Nora Surojegin is an author, illustrator and graphic designer from Finland. She enjoys creating imaginative worlds and her storytelling brims with whimsy and subtle humour.

Pirkko-Liisa and Nora, a talented mother–daughter team, also co-created the highly acclaimed storybook, *Otto and the Secret Light of Christmas*.

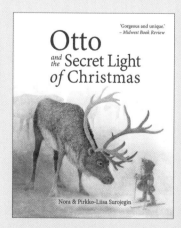

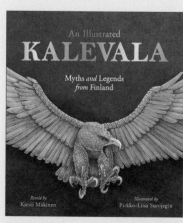